To:

From:

I Promise You

Marianne Richmond

SOURCEBOOKS
jabberwocky

Watercolor was used to prepare the full color art.

Published by Sourcebooks Jabberwocky, an imprint of Sourcebooks Kids
P.O. Box 4410, Naperville, Illinois 60567-4410
(630) 961-3900
sourcebookskids.com

Library of Congress Cataloging-in-Publication Data is on file with the publisher.

Source of Production: Worzalla-USA, Stevens Point, WI
Date of Production: July 2020
Run Number: 5019234

Printed and bound in the United States of America.
WOZ 10 9 8 7 6 5 4 3 2 1

To CAJW,
my four who
hold my promises.

When you first came to me, so little and new,
I held you close and rocked you slow
and made a *promise* to you.

I promise to **grow** you

and **show** you
with all of my heart,

I'm here for you **always**...

right from the start.

I promise you **roots**, a place to belong, where you can

be yourself freely and **learn** right from wrong.

I promise you **time**
for laughing and play
and to notice the moments
that bring fun to our day.

I promise you **choices** to bravely begin

to find
your own voice
and what lights
you within.

When your body is growing and you're full of knowing,
I promise you **limits** for your coming and going.

I promise you **help**
to figure things out,
when your mind is mixed-up
with question and doubt.

I promise you **guidance** and cheering
and hugs when you're fearing
waves that are tossing
the ship you are steering.

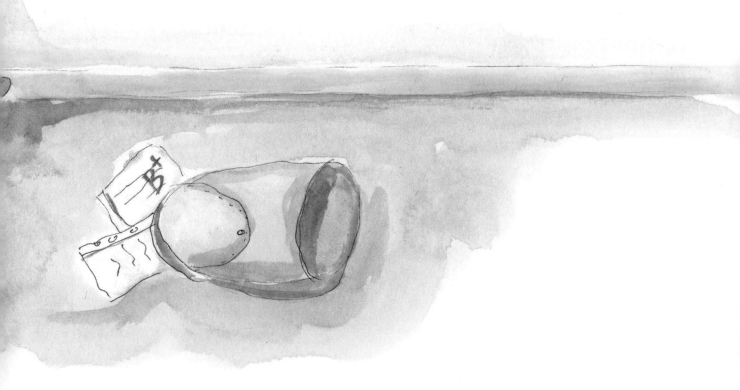

I can't promise you easy

or perfect or fair,

but I promise you *listening*
to the feelings you share.

I promise you **acceptance** of ways you're not me, even though we are part of the same family.

I promise you **truth** and
reminding of your infinite worth,
built-in and boundless
since your moment of birth.

When your wings are full-grown
and you fly from the nest,

I promise you *wishes*
for life's beauty and best.

I promise you **prayers** as you choose and explore,

and I promise you
home
in my heart
and in my door.

I promise you **love**
for your lifetime through.
Steady, endless, and sure...

This I *promise* you.

MARIANNE RICHMOND is a bestselling author and artist who has touched the lives of millions for more than two decades by creating books that celebrate the love of family. Visit her at mariannerichmond.com.

"My books help you share your heart and connect with those you love."

xo, M.